Tilly
the Teacher
Fairy

To all my inspiring teachers

Special thanks to
Rachel Elliot

ORCHARD BOOKS
338 Euston Road, London NW1 3BH
Orchard Books Australia
Level 17/207 Kent Street, Sydney, NSW 2000
A Paperback Original

First published in 2014 by Orchard Books

A CIP catalogue record for this book is available
from the British Library.

ISBN 978 1 40833 379 2

1 3 5 7 9 10 8 6 4 2

Printed in Great Britain

The paper and board used in this paperback are natural recyclable
products made from wood grown in sustainable forests. The
manufacturing processes conform to the environmental regulations
of the country of origin.

Orchard Books is a division of Hachette Children's Books,
an Hachette UK company

www.hachette.co.uk

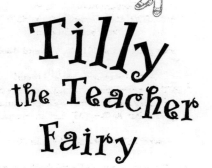

Tilly
the Teacher
Fairy

by Daisy Meadows

ORCHARD

www.rainbowmagic.co.uk

The Fairyland Palace

Queen Titania's Seeing Pool

Tippington Town

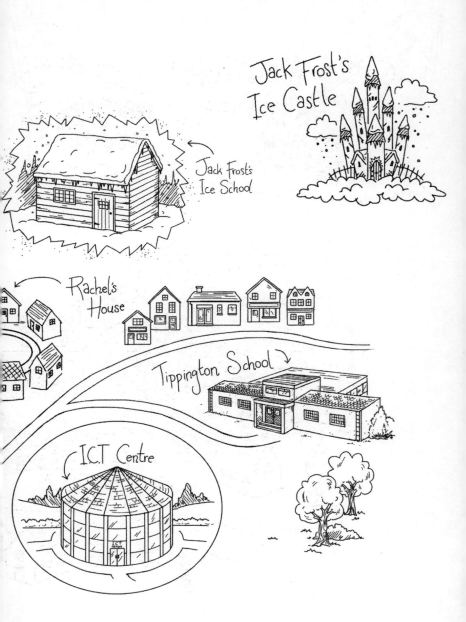

Jack Frost's
Ice Castle

Jack Frost's
Ice School

Rachel's
House

Tippington School

ICT Centre

Jack Frost's Spell

I think teachers shout and boss
And get their way by being cross.
So that's the perfect job for me.
I'll be as bad as bad can be.

Silly Tilly's much too nice
To teach the world of frost and ice.
She is helpful, kind and calm,
But I'll fill students with alarm!

The Fairy Laptop

Contents

A School Day Together

"I love the fact that I am actually
walking to school with you," said
Rachel Walker to her best friend Kirsty
Tate. "I wish we went to the same one
all the time."

"Me too," said Kirsty, linking arms
with Rachel. "But I'm excited to be here
even just for a day. It's such a special
occasion."

Ahead of them, lots of children were on their way to school. Everyone seemed hopeful and excited, and laughter filled the air. They had been waiting for this day for a very long time. At last, the school's dazzling new state-of-the-art ICT centre was about to open.

"We were fundraising for a whole year," Rachel remembered. "We did sponsored swims, cake sales and raffles."

"And a jumble sale and a sponsored read," Kirsty added. "I helped with those, remember?"

"I'll never forget that," said Rachel, squeezing her arm. "That's why you've been allowed a day off from your school to spend with me!"

Rachel and Kirsty had been best friends ever since they first met on Rainspell Island. Together, they had helped the Rainbow Fairies and had become secret friends with all of Fairyland.

"You're so lucky to have an ICT centre at last," Kirsty went on. "Everyone in your school will be able to use the latest computers, and you'll have training sessions, amazing presentations, films and writing workshops – it sounds brilliant!"

"It's not just us," Rachel added. "All the local schools are going to be allowed to use it. That's why they've all been invited to the opening ceremony."

Everyone was going to take part in a short ICT course, and at the end there would be a prize-giving ceremony to hand out the centre's first-ever certificates.

"I can't wait to see it," Kirsty said.

"It's taken a whole year to build, and nobody except the headmaster has been allowed to look inside," Rachel told her friend. "I think the teachers are as excited as we are to find out what it's like!"

"So tell me more about your teachers," Kirsty went on. "Which one's your favourite?"

"I really like Mr Pike," said Rachel. "He's so funny. And I think you'll like Mrs Bowler too – she's very kind."

Kirsty suddenly noticed that all the other children were ahead of them.

"Goodness, Rachel, we'll be late if we don't hurry up," she exclaimed. "Come on!"

Just then, the girls heard a bicycle bell ringing behind them. They turned and saw a lady with a helmet cycling towards them.

"No dawdling, girls," she called out. "You don't want to be late, today of all days!"

"That's Mrs Bowler," whispered Rachel. "She's quite strict but she's nice underneath."

The teacher cycled past them, and the girls watched her go. There was a pile of different-sized books strapped to the back of her bicycle, and suddenly something small and sparkly tumbled from the pile.

"Mrs Bowler, you've dropped
something!" called Rachel.

But the teacher didn't hear her. Rachel
started to call again, but Kirsty grabbed
her arm.

"Wait!" she said in a thrilled voice. "That's not a book. It's a fairy!"

Tilly's Tale

Luckily, none of the other children had turned around when Rachel shouted. The blonde-haired fairy zoomed towards them and landed on the palm of Kirsty's hand. She was wearing a pair of pink, cropped trousers and a silky blue blouse with a pussycat bow. Kirsty cupped her hands around the fairy and smiled at her.

"Hello," she said. "I'm Kirsty and this is my best friend Rachel."

"Oh, I know who you are," said the fairy. "Everyone in Fairyland knows how kind you are to us. That's why I'm here. I'm Tilly the Teacher Fairy, by the way. I look after teachers all over the human and fairy worlds."

"Hello, Tilly," said Rachel. "Has something happened?"

"Yes," Tilly replied, looking very upset.

"Jack Frost has stolen all my magical objects!"

Rachel and Kirsty exchanged worried looks.

"Can you tell us about it while we walk along?" Kirsty asked. "We really want to help, but we can't be late. Today is a very important day for Rachel's school."

"Of course," said Tilly. "I know all about the new media centre. That's why I need your help so much. Without my magical objects, the opening of your centre will be a disaster!"

She fluttered up to Rachel's shoulder and tucked herself under a lock of blonde hair. Arm in arm, the girls carried on walking while Tilly explained what had happened in Fairyland.

"You see, I was teaching a class of young fairies how to cast a vanishing spell," she explained. "They got a little bit overexcited, and one of them accidentally vanished my objects onto the roof."

Rachel gave a little giggle.

"Does that sort of thing happen a lot when you're teaching?" she asked.

Tilly laughed too.

"Yes, especially with vanishing spells," she said. "Usually it's easy to fix, but this time we had really bad luck. Just at the moment the objects appeared on the roof, Jack Frost was passing by with his goblins."

"Oh no," said Kirsty, instantly guessing the rest of the story. "He sent his goblins to steal them?"

"Exactly," said Tilly with a sigh. "The goblins clambered up to the roof and took the objects. Then Jack Frost zapped them onto a lightning cloud and they flew away before we could stop them."

"Oh, he is so mean!" said Rachel in a cross voice. "Why would he want to steal your things?"

"I asked him that," said Tilly. "He just

stood there and laughed at me! He said
that he was tired of teachers making
all the rules. He wants to decide what
happens in every classroom ever built."

"Oh my goodness, I don't like the
sound of that," said Kirsty. "What did
he mean?"

"I didn't get the chance to ask him,"
said Tilly. "He swished his wand and
disappeared in a flash of blue lightning. I
have no idea where he went — or where
he has hidden my magical objects!"

The girls had arrived at the school
gates, where there were lots of children
in the playground. They still had time to
talk about the news from Fairyland.

"What *are* your magical objects?"
Rachel asked.

"Well, there's the fairy laptop," Tilly

began. "That makes sure all teachers'
presentations go well. The magic apple
helps lessons to go smoothly, and the
enchanted folder keeps all official school
certificates in safe hands."

"What do you want us to do?" asked Kirsty. "How can we help?"

"Come with me to Fairyland," said Tilly at once. "I need to find Jack Frost, and I want to start at the Ice Castle. But I'm a bit scared to go there all by myself, and I know you've been before. Will you come with me?"

"Of course we will," Rachel said.

At that moment, the school bell rang. A tall teacher with a beard waved at Rachel and Kirsty.

"Come on, you two!" he called. "Chop-chop!"

"That's Mr Pike," said Rachel. "Tilly, we have to go to registration. We can't be late today!"

"Of course," said Tilly. "But find a quiet place as soon as you can. Then I'll take us all back to Fairyland. We have to stop Jack Frost!"

A Bucket, a Mop and Some Magic

Tilly slipped into Rachel's school bag, and the girls hurried towards the main entrance.

"I hope we're not late for registration," said Rachel.

"I don't think we need to worry about that!" said Kirsty as they walked inside.

The school was in uproar. Children
from different classes were running in all
directions, shouting and laughing.

"Is registration over?" Rachel asked.
"Why is everyone running around?
Where are all the teachers?"

A boy from her class was playing with a yo-yo nearby. He turned to look at her.

"Haven't you heard?" he said. "Every single computer in the new media centre has frozen. They all have pictures of snowflakes on blue screens, and the headmaster thinks it's a virus. All the teachers have gone over there to try to help. If they can't get the computers to work, there will be no opening ceremony today. Mr Pike said that registration will have to wait."

33

Rachel and Kirsty exchanged knowing glances. Freezing screens and pictures of snowflakes? This was the work of Jack Frost!

"Tilly, can you use your magic to fix the computers?" asked Kirsty in a low voice.

Tilly peeped up at them out of Rachel's bag.

"Not without my magical objects," she said. "The spells wouldn't be strong enough without the fairy laptop. I'm  sorry, but I can't do anything to fix the computers until I get it back."

Just then there was a loud shout and Mr Pike came striding down the corridor.

"Can't you all sit quietly for five minutes?" he demanded. "Everyone, back into your classrooms right now. This is not the kind of behaviour we want to see today!"

"Once we're inside the classroom, there'll be no way for us to help Tilly," Rachel whispered. "We won't have anywhere to hide."

"Then we have to hide right now," said Kirsty, spotting a half-open cupboard door. "*Come on!*"

She grabbed Rachel's hand and pulled her into the cupboard, pulling the door almost closed behind them. Then they held their breath, hoping that they hadn't been spotted. Outside the door, footsteps hurried along the corridor, but no one stopped. At last they heard the sound of classroom doors closing, and then there was silence.

It was very dark inside the cupboard. Even though the door was slightly ajar, the girls could hardly see each other.

"I think my foot's stuck in a bucket," Rachel whispered. "This is the caretaker's cupboard."

"I'm sitting on a soggy mop," said Kirsty with a giggle. "We can't stay in here for long."

Suddenly a tiny golden light appeared and floated upwards. It grew brighter, and the girls saw that it came from the tip of Tilly's wand.

"Everyone stay calm," she said in a rather teacher-like tone of voice. "It's time for a little magic."

In the darkness of the caretaker's cupboard, Tilly's wand glimmered when she waved it in the air. It left a rainbow shape of golden fairy dust, which hung in the air for a moment and then sprinkled down on the girls.

"Now we're glimmering too," said Rachel in delight.

She held out her arm, which was shining with fairy dust. Kirsty seemed to be glowing gold. As Rachel watched, her best friend became smaller and smaller, until she was the same size as Tilly. Then Rachel realised that she was shrinking too. In a few moments, they were all hovering in mid air. Their wings were moving so fast that they were just shimmering blurs.

"All of a sudden this cupboard seems enormous," said Kirsty with a laugh.

"Hold hands, girls," said Tilly. "We're going to Fairyland."

Jack Frost's Notes

Tilly swished her wand upwards and took Kirsty's hand. Rachel and Kirsty had already twined their fingers together. They heard a far-off sound, like the tinkling of a thousand silver bells, and then the cupboard was filled with a dazzling light. The girls squeezed their eyes shut, and felt a frosty gust of wind ruffle their hair. When they opened their

eyes, they found themselves fluttering
beside a grim, grey castle wall. They had
reached the coldest place in Fairyland –
the Ice Castle, Jack Frost's home.

"Brrr, we're going to need some
warmer clothes," said Tilly.

She waved her
wand and
gave each
of them
a fleecy
hooded
jacket in
a different
colour.
Kirsty gladly
pulled up
her hood and
gazed around.

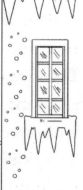

"That's funny," she said after a moment. "There are no guards on duty."

Rachel looked up at the turrets and flew closer to the wooden entrance gate. Everywhere was completely deserted.

"You're right," she said with a puzzled frown. "There isn't a single goblin in sight."

"But look at the gate," Tilly said, pointing at it. "There's a note attached. Let's go and see what it says."

"Wait," said Kirsty. "It could be a trap."

"I don't think that the goblins are that cunning," said Rachel. "But get ready to fly fast if they suddenly appear!"

Trying to look around in all directions, Tilly, Rachel and Kirsty flew up to the gate. The note was written on a scrap of paper torn from a school homework book.

> TO WHATEVER PESKY FAIRIES WHAT TURN UP, ESPECIALLY THAT BOSSY TEACHER FAIRY!
>
> You won't never find me or the magical objects either ha ha ha so you might as well GIVE UP and GO HOME. And I am millions cleverer than what you are, so GO AWAY!

Tilly shook her head and made a tutting noise.

"Someone needs to give Jack Frost a lesson in manners," she said. "Not to mention grammar!"

"Look down here," said Rachel, landing on the ice-covered cobbles in front of the gate.

A folded note was pinned to the

bottom of the gate. Rachel bent down, removed the pin and carried the note up to Kirsty and Tilly. It had the words 'For Goblin Eyes Only' written on the front.

"I think we should look at this," said Tilly.

She took the note and unfolded it. Rachel and Kirsty read it over her shoulder.

You're late, you nincompoop! Follow the blue footprints through the woods. HURRY UP!

Kirsty gazed down at the frosty cobblestones. At the very corner of the castle she caught a glimpse of a blue shape.

"Down there!" she cried.

She zoomed towards the castle corner,

closely followed by Rachel and Tilly.
Now she could see that the blue shape
was a sparkling footprint.

"There's another!" said Rachel,
pointing further ahead. "And another…
and another!"

"Let's follow them," said Tilly.

Rachel and Kirsty were already flying ahead. The magical blue footprints led around the castle and across an overgrown lawn. They disappeared into a thicket of bushes.

"Those thorny bushes will hurt our wings," said Rachel. "Let's fly over them. Perhaps the footprints come out the other side."

But when the three friends fluttered over the bushes, they saw something far more interesting than blue footprints. A flimsy-looking wooden building was standing in a clearing. There was a large sign outside that made Tilly gasp and hover in the air.

JACK FROST'S ICE SCHOOL
MOTTO: DO YOUR WORST!

Rachel, Kirsty and Tilly fluttered down to the building and hovered below an icicle-edged windowsill. Looking up, they could see ice on the inside of the window too.

"Let's look inside," whispered Kirsty. Slowly, they fluttered upwards just enough to let them peer over the windowsill.

"Oh my goodness," said Rachel with a gasp.

The room was packed with goblins!

School for Scamps

The goblins were sitting at tables, on tables and under tables, and every single one of them was fidgeting. Jack Frost was standing at one end of the room, and a pink laptop was open on the desk in front of him. One bony hand was resting on the keyboard as he talked.

"That's it!" said Tilly. "That's my magic laptop!"

"Brilliant," said Kirsty. "But how are we going to get it back?"

"Shh," said Rachel. "Let's listen to what he's saying."

The walls and windows were so thin that it was easy to hear what Jack Frost was saying. As usual, he was ranting in a loud voice.

"You lot need to learn a few lessons," he was saying. "Let's get one thing straight. This is my classroom and I'm the teacher, so you have to do whatever I say. And if anybody disobeys, I'll put you in detention for a year!"

"This sounds like the start of a lesson," said Tilly. "We could be waiting for ages before they leave the classroom – and then he will probably take the magic laptop with him."

"We're not giving in," said Rachel in a determined voice.

"What's the one thing that always, always gets everyone out of a classroom fast — even in the middle of a lesson?"

Tilly looked puzzled, but Kirsty's eyes lit up at once.

"Fire drill!" she exclaimed.

"Exactly," said Rachel. "Tilly, can you set off a fire alarm?"

"Easy as pie," said Tilly, with a wink. "You had better cover your ears."

She raised her wand and gave it a flick.

At once, the deafening sound of a fire alarm shook the windows of the wooden classroom.

All the icicles fell off the windowsill, and inside the goblins sprang to their feet.

"Fire!" they squawked. "Help! Help!"

"Nobody panic," said a tall goblin in a bossy voice. "I'm the fire monitor today. Everyone outside, now. No running, jumping or pushing."

The fairies hid under the classroom steps as the goblins trooped out, followed by a very grumpy-looking Jack Frost. The tall goblin had found a clipboard from somewhere, and was licking the end of a stubby pencil.

"I have to call the fire register to check you're all here," he shouted in a bossy voice. "Jack Frost?"

"Here," growled Jack Frost.

"Goblin one?"

"Here!"

"Goblin two?"

"Here!"

"Pimply Goblin?"

"Here!"

"Short Plump Goblin?"

"Here!"

"Tall Plump Goblin?"

"Here!"

"Come on!"

whispered Kirsty.

The classroom
door was open,
so it was easy
for them to
fly inside. Tilly
zoomed over to the
laptop, landed gently
beside it and picked
it up.

"Hurray!" Rachel cried.

But at that moment, they heard a
furious yell of rage.

"I didn't *install* a fire alarm!" bellowed
Jack Frost.

He was standing in the doorway,
blocking their exit, his eyes blazing.

"My goblins have surrounded this building," he said with a sneer. "Give me that laptop."

"It doesn't belong to you," said Rachel, as Tilly clutched the laptop to her chest.

"I don't care about that," Jack Frost bawled. "I want it! You can't escape, so you might as well hand it over."

Rachel and Kirsty exchanged worried looks.

"What are we going to do?" Kirsty whispered. "He's bigger and stronger than us."

"That's true," said Tilly with a twinkle in her eye. "But any good teacher will tell you that brains can always outwit brawn."

"What do you mean?" asked Rachel.

"I mean that if you think about it logically, there's only one way out," Tilly whispered. "Going UP!"

She pointed her wand at the roof, and part of it seemed to dissolve away. Jack Frost bounded towards them, but he was too late. The three fairies went shooting upwards through the roof.

"This way to the Fairyland Palace!" cried Tilly.

The Magic
Apple

Contents

A Royal Welcome

Tilly led Rachel and Kirsty away from Jack Frost's Ice Castle as fast as they could fly. They zoomed over snow-tipped fir trees and frozen streams. Gradually the frost and ice gave way to green grass and summery breezes, and they saw toadstool houses and fairy glades below them. At last they saw the pink turrets of the Fairyland Palace glittering ahead of them. Gladly, they pulled off their warm fleeces and landed beside the entrance.

"That was exciting!" said Rachel.

"I was a bit scared at the end," Kirsty admitted with a little smile.

"But I got my fairy laptop back," said Tilly, hugging it to her chest. "I'm really starting to believe that Jack Frost won't get away with this after all."

"Of course he won't," said Rachel, giving her arm a comforting squeeze.

Just then, the grand door opened and the fairies gasped. The king and queen of Fairyland were standing before them. Rachel, Kirsty and Tilly curtseyed, and Queen Titania held out her arms in a wide welcome.

"Thank you, Rachel and Kirsty," she said. "Once again you have come to our aid. We are so grateful to you."

"We are always happy to help," said Kirsty.

"I'm afraid we must ask you to help even more," the queen went on. "Jack Frost still has two of Tilly's magical objects, and we are all worried. An old friend of yours has been to see me."

She moved aside, and a fairy stepped out from behind her.

"Carly the Schoolfriend Fairy!" Rachel exclaimed. "It's lovely to see you!"

Carly hurried forward and hugged her friends.

"I've been so worried about the missing magic apple," she said. "But now I know that you're helping us, I'm sure

that everything's going to be all right."

"Why are you worried about the magic apple?" Kirsty asked.

"Lessons will be spoiled without it," said Carly. "Teachers will lose control of their classes. They will forget their lesson plans. Fairy lessons are already going wrong, and I'm sure the same is happening in the human world."

"Carly's right," said Tilly to the girls.

"Now we have the fairy laptop back, the IT problems at your school will be over. But lots of things could still go wrong for the grand opening."

"We'll do everything we can to find the magic apple," Rachel promised.

"My magic pool might be able to help," said Queen Titania. "At least it could show us where Jack Frost is now, and perhaps we will get a clue about the magic apple."

The queen led them through the palace gardens, her silver dress swishing over the grass. When they reached the Seeing Pool, she waved her wand over it. The girls drew in their breath as the water began to shimmer in all the colours of the rainbow. They had seen the Pool many times, but it was still thrilling to see the picture form on the surface of the water.

Jack Frost was standing in his classroom, facing rows of sleepy-looking goblins. He was holding up a red, shiny apple. Tilly let out a cry of excitement.

"That's it!" she exclaimed. "That's my magic apple!"

The Perfect Present

"Now listen to me, you bunch of squawking toerags," Jack Frost barked. "This is that rotten fairy's magic apple, and a smart goblin could make all sorts of mischief with it. So who wants it?"

"Me! Me!" shrieked every goblin in the room, making Kirsty clap her hands over her ears.

"Well, TOUGH, because you can't get something for nothing," Jack Frost snapped. "In the human world, pupils give their teachers apples to show how much they appreciate everything they've learned. Well, I've taught you everything you know! So I deserve a present too. And the goblin who gives me the best present will win this amazing magic apple."

A short and pimply goblin put up his hand.

"What?" bellowed Jack Frost.

"What present do you want?" asked the goblin in a squeaky voice.

Jack Frost's eyes narrowed and his lips curled. "That is the *challenge*, you idiot!"

The queen swished her wand and the picture disappeared. She looked at Kirsty and Rachel.

"Do you have any ideas, girls?" she asked.

"Well," said Kirsty, "the easiest way to get the magic apple from Jack Frost is for him to give it to us."

"He'll never do that!" exclaimed Tilly.

The queen held up her hand.

"Wait, Tilly," she said with a little smile. "I think Kirsty has an idea."

She nodded at Kirsty, who took a deep breath.

"I think we should disguise ourselves as goblins," she said. "We could make sure that we give Jack Frost the most amazing present he can imagine. Then he'll give us the magic apple – hopefully!"

"Kirsty, that's a wonderful idea!" cried Tilly.

"I agree," said Carly. "It'll work perfectly – as long as we can think of a good enough present."

"But what do you give to an Ice Lord who is never happy with anything?" asked Rachel with a frown.

The queen clapped her hands together to summon Bertram, the Royal Frog Footman. He sprang out of a bush and the girls jumped in surprise. Bertram gave a deep bow.

"Please gather as many fairies as you can in the grand meeting hall," said the queen. "We're going to need help to think of the perfect present."

Bertram bowed again and hurried away. He must have worked very quickly, because by the time the queen had led Rachel and Kirsty to the grand meeting hall, it was half-filled with fairies. The king was striding up and down, rubbing his beard thoughtfully. Every time a fairy had an idea, she pointed her wand at a large white board and wrote the idea in colourful, sparkling letters. There were already lots of ideas on the board.

An icicle that can never melt.
A new cloak that changes colour when Jack Frost clicks his fingers.
A pet kitten that can speak to Jack Frost.
A magical book that tells Jack Frost when it's snowing in the human world.

A miniature snow globe model of the Ice Castle with tiny moving models of Jack Frost and the goblins.

Carly read the ideas out loud. "What do you think?" she asked Rachel and Kirsty.

"I'm not sure," said Kirsty. "I can imagine Jack Frost being rude about them all, just for fun."

Suddenly Rachel clapped her hands together.

"I think I've got it!" she cried. "It's got to be something big to impress Jack Frost – he always thinks that bigger means better. Well, the internet is the biggest thing I can think of, so how about we build a fan website all about Jack Frost?"

"Yes!" Tilly exclaimed. "Perfect! Jack Frost loves things that are all about him."

Kirsty gave a shiver.

"That's why it's so important to be careful on the internet," she said seriously. "It'd be scary to stumble across a fansite all about Jack Frost!"

Jack Frost's Fansite

The king and queen looked hopeful, and all the fairies gathered around in excitement.

"Do you know how to build a website?" Tilly asked Rachel.

"No, I'm sorry," said Rachel. "That's one of the things I'm hoping to learn in my school's new ICT centre."

"Don't worry," said Carly. "If Tilly and I combine our magic, we can build the fan website of Jack Frost's dreams!"

Tilly and Carly used their magic to create a silvery-blue laptop, which they could give to Jack Frost. Then Rachel, Kirsty and the fairies started to create an adoring website all about Jack Frost.

They devoted a whole page to his hair and another to his fashion sense. They created links where fans could buy clothes from his Ice Blue designer range. They wrote about his fantastic singing voice and used the music of the Gobolicious Band as the website theme tune.

"How about a page of recipes?" Kirsty suggested. "Iced buns and frosted cupcakes."

"Ooh yes," said Rachel. "Chilled jelly and ice cream!"

The fairies started adding their ideas for pages.

"How to be more like Jack Frost," suggested Una the Concert Fairy.

"A fan message board," called out Keira the Film Star Fairy.

"Jack Frost's biggest adventures," Elisa the Adventure Fairy proposed.

"A photo gallery," added Brooke the Photographer Fairy.

"Jack Frost's funniest quotes," said Libby the Story-Writing Fairy with a giggle.

Everyone was surprised to find that they were having fun.

"This is making me even more excited about the new ICT centre," Rachel whispered to Kirsty. "Imagine how much fun it would be to build a real website!"

At last the website was completed. All the fairies cheered and clapped as Tilly tucked the laptop under her arm.

"There's no time to
lose," she said,
giving the girls
a determined
look. "Are
you ready?"

"Ready
to become
goblins?"
asked Kirsty.
"As ready as I'll
ever be!"

Queen Titania gazed around the room.
"Many thanks to all you fairies who
have helped us here today," she said
in her silvery voice. "Now it is time to
leave Rachel, Kirsty and Tilly alone to
get ready for their adventure."

Waving and smiling, the fairies left the meeting room. Queen Titania rested her hands on the girls' shoulders.

"Good luck," she said. "The king and I will watch you in the Seeing Pool."

"Don't worry," said Rachel, sounding braver than she felt. "We'll get that magic apple back for Tilly."

When they were alone in the meeting room, Tilly raised her wand and swished it above their heads. Kirsty saw Rachel's skin slowly turning green, and bubbling up with spots and warts. Her hair disappeared, and her ears and nose grew long and pointy. Kirsty reached up to stroke her own hair and found that it had been replaced with a bald, bumpy head. They had been transformed into goblins!

"We all look exactly the same," said Kirsty in a goblin squawk.

"We even sound the same," Rachel added. "How are we going to tell each other apart?"

"Aha," said Tilly with a wink. "This is an idea that Miley the Stylist Fairy gave me!"

With a flick of her wand, a purple scarf appeared around Kirsty's neck. Rachel had a yellow bobble hat and Tilly had a pair of pink fluffy ear warmers and a pink rucksack.

"There," she said, tucking the laptop into her rucksack. "Just don't forget what each of us is wearing."

The three friends smiled at each other and linked arms. Then Tilly waved her wand, and in a burst of sparkles they were transported to the door of Jack Frost's classroom.

"Time to start acting like goblins," Tilly whispered. "Everything depends on us now!"

Top of the Class

Rachel knocked on the classroom door as Tilly tucked her wand into her handbag.

"Remember, you have to be a bit rude if you're going to sound like a real goblin," Kirsty whispered.

The door was flung open by a
grumpy-faced goblin with a wonky tie
around his neck.

"What do you want?" he snapped.

"We've got a present for Jack Frost,"
said Rachel. "Let us in."

"Join the queue," said the goblin,
jerking his thumb over his shoulder.

The three fake goblins walked into the classroom and saw a line of real goblins waiting beside the teacher's desk. Each of them was holding a badly wrapped gift. Jack Frost was sitting at the desk, and there was a pile of discarded presents behind him. As the disguised fairies joined the queue, they saw him toss another present over his shoulder.

"Another toaster!" he roared. "What do I want with a stupid toaster? I don't even *like* toast!"

At that, five goblins hurriedly left the queue clutching toaster-shaped parcels.

"A teacher like me deserves a GOOD present!" Jack Frost moaned.

As the fairies waited their turn, they saw one goblin after another try to please Jack Frost with a gift. But time after time, presents were flung over the Ice Lord's shoulder.

"Boring!" he shouted. "Old-fashioned! Stupid!"

The classroom was filled with the sound of goblin knees knocking together.

"Who's going to give him the present?" Tilly whispered in a nervous voice.

The girls looked at each other. No one really wanted to do it, because by now Jack Frost was in a very bad mood indeed.

"I'll do it," said Rachel after a pause. "After all, it was my idea. If it all goes wrong, I should face it."

Kirsty squeezed Rachel's hand.

"We'll all face it together," she said.

At last it was their turn. Rachel stepped forward, opened the laptop and placed it in front of Jack Frost. His face was like thunder.

"A laptop?" he bawled. "A laptop? After that prissy little fairy took my laptop away? I never want to see another laptop as long as I live, you straw-brained nincompoop!"

Rachel was so scared that she couldn't speak. But Kirsty hurried forward.

"This is something extra special," she said, pressing a button to show him the fansite. "Look — it's all about you."

Jack stared at the screen as the Gobolicious Band music began to play. A picture of himself appeared.

"Have a look through the site," Tilly said in an encouraging voice. "There are lots of pages."

Jack Frost stretched out a long, bony finger and clicked through the website. As he found each new page, his eyes seemed to grow bigger and bigger.

"It's beautiful," he whispered. "The most beautiful thing I have ever seen."

Tilly, Rachel and Kirsty exchanged happy glances. The plan was working!

"At last the world will know what it means to be a true star,"

Jack Frost went on, gazing at the recipes page. "They will all be talking about my talent, my looks, my wisdom. I'll have my own range of frozen ready meals. I'll write a cookery book. I'll star in my own reality TV show. Nothing can stop me now!"

He hadn't said a word of thanks to the girls, but they hadn't expected it.

"Does that mean we win the prize?" asked Tilly in a timid voice.

"Yes, you can have the stupid apple," said Jack Frost. "I don't know what it does anyway."

He pulled the magic apple from his pocket and held it out to them. With her heart thumping, Tilly leaned forward to take it.

A Thoughtless Spell

As Tilly leaned forward, her handbag slipped sideways and the tip of her wand stuck out of it. Even then, Jack Frost only had eyes for his website. But Tilly's wand was now so close to the Ice Lord that it gave a little tinkle of alarm, and Jack Frost looked up.

"What's that?" he roared.

His fingers closed around the apple and snatched it back.

"It's nothing," Tilly stammered, pushing the wand down. "Just something we…er…"

"You can't fool me!" Jack Frost yelled. "This is some sort of fairy trick – I know it! Well, you won't get away with it this time!"

He stood up and gave a vicious flick of his wand, snapping out a spell as he did so.

By icy winds and splintery sticks,
Undo all fairy spells and tricks.
Let fairy magic all be lost
Inside this room with great Jack Frost!

A freezing blast of wind shot through the classroom. With a loud pop, Tilly became a fairy again. Rachel and Kirsty gaped at each other. They were still fairy size, but they didn't have any wings!

"We're human," said Rachel with a gasp. "But how… why…?"

"Jack Frost has destroyed all fairy magic inside this room," said Tilly. "You are still fairy size because no one of human size can enter Fairyland. But his magic has removed your wings as well as our disguise."

"What are we going to do?" cried Kirsty.

"I don't think that Jack Frost has quite thought this through," said Rachel in a low voice.

She turned her gaze to the laptop. Even as Jack Frost was cackling with laughter, his precious fansite started to collapse. The pages of photographs and articles turned into meaningless strings of numbers that melted away before his eyes. Then the laptop itself shimmered and began to disappear. Jack Frost's

laughter turned into a strangled choke of
rage and panic. He flung himself at the
vanishing laptop, and the apple fell from
his hand, forgotten.

"Quick!" cried Tilly.

Kirsty dived towards the apple and skidded halfway across the classroom on her stomach, reaching out her hands in front of her. She grabbed the apple and stumbled to her feet. Rachel was close behind her, pulling her towards the door.

"You got it!" she shouted. "RUN!"

They heard a scream of rage, and then lightning bolts blasted around them as they hurtled out of the classroom. Tilly used her wand to send the lightning bolts sideways and then zoomed after them, looping the loop through the air so that the lightning bolts couldn't hit her.

She slammed the door behind her and locked it with a flick of her wand. Rachel and Kirsty had collapsed onto the grass outside, panting.

"We got it!" said Kirsty, holding up the magic apple in delight.

The three friends shared a hug,
and then Rachel pointed to the
classroom. A crowd of goblins was
cowering beside the windows, their
breath steaming up the glass. Behind
them, Jack Frost was still setting off
lightning bolts in a furious temper.

"Goodness, I think we should go before
he escapes," said Rachel.

Tilly winked and raised her wand.

"Just one more magical object to find," she said happily. "Oh girls, we've almost done it! But first, I must take you back to the human world. I can't replace your wings while we are in Fairyland."

There was a sparkly flash, and then all the goblins gasped. Tilly, Rachel

and Kirsty had disappeared in a puff of
glittering fairy dust.

The Enchanted Folder

Contents

Back in the Broom Cupboard

When the sparkles faded, Rachel and Kirsty saw that they were back in the gloom of the caretaker's cupboard at school. No time had passed since Tilly took them to Fairyland, but now there were no shouts or running footsteps in the corridor outside.

"I must return the magic apple to the Fairyland School," said Tilly. "And you must both hurry to your classroom – it's registration time!"

"But what about the enchanted folder?" asked Rachel. "We still have to find that to make sure Jack Frost doesn't ruin everything."

"I'll come back and see you later," Tilly promised.

Suddenly the girls saw the door move. Someone was coming into the cupboard! Tilly disappeared with a little 'pop', and Rachel and Kirsty stood up very straight. The door opened and they saw the caretaker glaring down at them, his bushy eyebrows knitted together.

"Nothing but trouble today," said the caretaker in a grumpy voice. "If

it's not one thing it's another. First all
the computers freeze, and then I get the
blame for knocking over a keyboard
when I was cleaning the new ICT suite.
It was an accident! Now I have to put
up with pupils turning up in my cleaning
cupboard! Get along to your classroom
now, hurry up."

"Sorry, Mr Mason," said Rachel.

They slipped out of the cupboard and dashed along the corridor to Rachel's classroom. As they went, they could hear Mr Mason still grumbling to himself.

Before they could reach Rachel's room, all the classroom doors opened and the other pupils started walking out in pairs.

Rachel and Kirsty
joined them as
they lined up
beside the
doors to the
playground.
Mr Pike
clapped his
hands together.

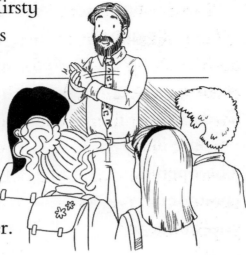

"All right,
everyone, listen
carefully. The Mayor has arrived to
perform the opening ceremony, the TV
cameras are outside and the crowds
are gathering. This is one of the most
exciting days in the history of Tippington
School! So today it's your job to be on
your best behaviour and show everyone
what our school is made of."

Rachel and
Kirsty exchanged
worried
glances.
There was
no time left!
The opening
ceremony
was about to
start, and one of
Tilly the Teacher

Fairy's magical objects
was still missing. Without the enchanted
folder, official school certificates could
be lost or damaged. Today of all days,
that would be a disaster! Later there was
going to be a prize-giving ceremony
to hand out the centre's first-ever
certificates. If the girls didn't find the

enchanted folder before then, everything was going to go terribly wrong.

Uninvited Pupils

Mr Pike opened the doors and everyone filed out into the playground. There was a huge crowd of people in front of the new ICT centre. Cameras flashed and whirred, and the Mayor stepped forward. Her official golden chains were draped around her neck, and she looked very important.

"Please put your hands together for the wonderful pupils of Tippington School," she said.

There was a loud burst of applause, and then the Mayor moved to stand in front of the ICT centre. A red ribbon had been stretched across the doors, and the Mayor took a pair of scissors out of her pocket.

"After two years of fundraising and waiting, these dedicated pupils are finally seeing their dream come true," she said. "It must be a truly magical day for them, and I feel honoured to have been asked to take part in it. It is with great pleasure that I declare the Tippington Information and Communication Technology Centre OPEN!"

With a loud snip, the red ribbon fluttered to the ground and the crowd cheered. The headmaster went to join the Mayor.

"I would like to invite all pupils to take part in a short introductory ICT course," he said in a booming voice. Please come in!"

As the cameras continued to flash, Rachel, Kirsty and all the other pupils walked into the new building, feeling very excited. For a  moment, they forgot all about Jack Frost and his naughty goblins.

"It's beautiful," said Rachel with a gasp.

Kirsty gazed around at the gleaming surfaces and brand-new carpet.

"Everything smells so fresh and clean," she said.

"This way to the auditorium," said the headmaster. "Our ICT teacher, Mr Nutbeam, is waiting to give you all your first lesson."

The new auditorium was brightly lit. Every row of seats was on a different level, and each seat had its own little table. Mr Nutbeam was standing on a stage behind a podium, and he waved at the pupils as they walked in.

"Let's sit here," said Rachel.

She took Kirsty's hand and they found seats in the middle of the auditorium. Mr Nutbeam started his lesson straight away.

"I'm going to give you an introduction to website building," he told them. "By the end of this class, you will be able to make a start on building your very own website."

Rachel and Kirsty shared a secret smile, remembering how they had helped the fairies build a website for Jack Frost.

At first, everything seemed to be going well. Mr Nutbeam had plenty of interesting tips, and Rachel and Kirsty made lots of notes.

"I can't wait to try this out at home," Rachel whispered. "Maybe we could make a website about Fairyland!"

Kirsty didn't reply, and Rachel gave her a little nudge.

"Don't you think it's exciting?" she asked.

Kirsty turned to her and put her finger to her lips. Then she pointed into a shadowy corner of the auditorium. At first, Rachel couldn't see anything. But when she screwed up her eyes, she could just make out a short, plump figure with pointy ears.

"It can't be!" she said with a gasp.

Kirsty nudged her again, and pointed at the door of the auditorium. A mischievous green face was peeping around it. The best friends stared at each other with wide eyes.

There were goblins in Rachel's school!

Lurking in the Shadows

Kirsty and Rachel found it very hard
to concentrate on the rest of the lesson.
How many goblins were in the school?
Why were they here? The girls only
noticed that Mr Nutbeam had finished
the lesson when the other pupils started
to clap.

"Thank you, everyone," he said.
"Now, each of you has a short test
in front of you, which should be easy
to complete if you've been listening.
You've got five minutes and then I'll
collect them."

The girls felt worried – they hadn't
been paying attention towards the end!
But luckily they had heard enough
to answer most of the questions, and
building the website with the fairies had
helped too. Mr Nutbeam collected the
papers and started to mark them.

"Why would goblins have come here?"
asked Kirsty in a low voice.

"It *must* have something to do with
the missing enchanted folder," Rachel
replied. "But I can't think what. It
doesn't make sense."

Kirsty glanced at Mr Nutbeam. He was frowning and tapping his head, almost as if he was trying to remember something. Then he reached out to the folder on his desk. He opened it and then frowned. He shook it upside down.

"Do you think he's having trouble marking the papers?" she asked Rachel.

"It looks as if something is missing," said Rachel.

Mr Nutbeam stood up.

"I'm very sorry, but I seem to have mislaid the certificates," he said.

"The presentation will have to wait. Please go back to your classrooms. Well done, everyone!"

While the other pupils left the auditorium, Rachel and Kirsty hung back. Mr Pike had been listening to the lesson, and he went to speak to Mr Nutbeam.

"Is everything all right?" he asked.

"I feel as if my brain is full of cotton wool," said Mr Nutbeam. "I just can't think of the right answers to this test."

"I'm the same this morning," said Mr Pike in a quiet voice. "I was trying to mark homework and I just couldn't do it. Must be all the excitement of the new building opening."

Rachel pulled Kirsty out of the auditorium.

"It's not excitement that's stopping the teachers from doing their jobs," she said. "It's all because we haven't got the enchanted folder back from Jack Frost."

They were the last pupils to leave the ICT centre. As they stepped out into the playground, they saw a spindly green leg disappear around the side of the main school building.

"That was a goblin," said Kirsty. "Come on, we have to follow him!"

They sprinted around the corner and saw a trail of litter stretching out in front of them. The girls stopped and picked up a couple of screwed-up pieces of paper.

"Certificates!" cried Rachel. "Oh Kirsty, these are Mr Nutbeam's certificates, and they've all been drawn on!"

The girls walked along, picking up the spoiled certificates. They had all been scribbled on and rewritten. Kirsty read one out.

Tall Pimply Goblin

is awarded a Diploma in Ice Castle Trickery (ICT)

Signed *Jack Frost*

Professor of ICT

The trail of crumpled certificates led the girls to the staff room. The door was half open, and they could hear loud squawks and screeches coming from inside.

"The teachers must be in the classrooms," said Kirsty. "It sounds as if the room is full of goblins. What shall we do?"

Rachel peeped around the door and gasped. Goblins were leaping across chairs and tables, ripping pages out of books and giggling in high-pitched voices.

"We have to stop them," she exclaimed. "They're going to ruin the staff room!"

Together, the best friends flung the door open wide and dashed in to the room.

"Stop it!" they cried.

But the goblins just sniggered and carried on. Then the girls heard the door close behind them, and the goblins cackled with laughter. With a feeling of dread, Rachel and Kirsty turned around. Jack Frost was standing between them and the door!

A Very Noisy Staff Room

"You interfering little humans are very, very annoying," said Jack Frost, pointing his wand at them. "I could blast you with lightning bolts right now for getting in the way of my plans."

Rachel squeezed Kirsty's hand, hoping that she had noticed the glowing folder tucked under Jack Frost's arm.

"That's Tilly's enchanted folder," Kirsty whispered. "It must be."

"We have to think of a way to get it back," said Rachel. "We can't let Tilly down."

Luckily the goblins were making so much noise that the girls could speak without being heard. Rachel looked around the room, trying to think of a way to stop the goblins destroying it. But they were everywhere, jumping on furniture, tearing

up paper, ripping books and scribbling on walls. The doors of a large cupboard were swinging open, and she could see a box inside. There was something about it that caught her eye.

"That's the confiscated items box," she whispered to Kirsty. "I've seen it before. It's where the teachers put things that pupils aren't supposed to bring into school."

"It looks almost as if it's glowing," said Kirsty.

"Stop muttering to each other!" Jack Frost yelled, as goblins rampaged around him. "What are you saying?"

Rachel shrugged, but her sharp eyes had spotted something. A tiny pair of sparkling eyes was peeping over the edge of the confiscated items box, and she could see gleaming blonde hair and the tips of two gossamer wings. She hid a little smile.

ISCATED S BOX

"It's Tilly," she whispered to Kirsty.

Tilly held her finger up to her lips. She had spotted the enchanted folder too, and the girls could tell that she had a plan. The little fairy fluttered out of the cupboard and zipped around behind Jack Frost. She pointed to her mouth, and Kirsty guessed what she meant.

"She wants us to keep him talking," she said. "We need to make sure he and the goblins keep looking this way."

153

Rachel pulled Kirsty around to face her.

"Clapping game," she said. "Say the words as loud as you can."

Kirsty and Rachel knew lots of clapping games, and they were very fast! They started to clap and sing, and Jack Frost stared at them in amazement and confusion. He had never seen anything like it.

"What are you doing?" he roared.

"They've gone barmy," said a goblin who was sitting on top of a filing cabinet.

"Stop it!" bellowed Jack Frost, hopping up and down with rage.

Rachel and Kirsty just sang louder and clapped harder. The goblins stared at them, and Jack Frost went purple with fury. He hated anything that he couldn't understand, and he couldn't understand this. He was too cross to notice Tilly fluttering up behind him.

As they sang, the girls watched Tilly out of the corners of their eyes. She was now just an arm's reach away from the enchanted folder, but she had stopped in mid-air. Kirsty thought that she understood. It was scary to be so close to Jack Frost, and it was even scarier to be trying to take something away from him. Kirsty guessed that Tilly was trying to feel brave.

Just then, as they were about to start a new song, the girls heard something. It sounded like chattering voices, and it was getting louder. They stopped clapping and heard footsteps in the corridor outside.

"The teachers are coming back!" cried Kirsty.

Rachel looked around the vandalised staff room.

"Oh no," she said with a groan.

156

"What will they do when they see this?"

Jack Frost gave a mean laugh and curled his lip.

"That's not my problem," he said. "Goblins, make more mess!"

In the Nick of Time

The teachers' footsteps were at the far end of the corridor, which meant that the girls only had a couple of minutes to get the enchanted folder back. But both Rachel and Kirsty could see that Tilly was too nervous to grab it.

"It's now or never," said Rachel to herself.

She took a deep breath and then ran
straight towards Jack Frost. He was so
surprised that he couldn't move or even
raise his wand. Rachel knocked the
wand out of his hand and yanked the
folder from under his arm. Jack Frost
gave a squeal and the goblins shrieked
with laughter.

Jack Frost scrabbled around on the floor, searching for his wand. When he had found it, he staggered to his feet and glared at Rachel and Kirsty.

"Give me that folder!" he snapped. "Thieves!"

"*You're* the thief," said Kirsty.

Tilly fluttered
over and
landed on
Kirsty's
shoulder.

"You took my
magical objects,
and now I've got
them back," she
said. "You should be
ashamed of yourself. I think you should
go straight back to your Ice Castle and
think about what you've done."

"I'll make you sorry!" Jack Frost
screeched. "I'll make you *all* sorry!"

He swept his wand around the
room and every single goblin
disappeared, leaving a little green
cloud puff in the air.

"I would be a better teacher than any silly human!" Jack Frost snarled. "Just you wait and see!"

He vanished with a final sneer and a crackling blue lightning bolt. There was no time to celebrate – the teachers' footsteps and voices were getting closer.

Rachel handed the folder to Tilly and it immediately shrank to fairy size.

"How on earth are we going to explain this mess?" asked Kirsty.

"I've got a special kind of magic for moments like this," said Tilly with a little smile.

She fluttered into the centre of the room and swished her wand from corner to corner. The ripped books were mended, tables were picked up and papers were repaired. Even the spoiled certificates were made as good as new and placed in a folder on the table.

"Now you must hurry back to the ICT centre," said Tilly. "As soon as the teachers find the certificates, everything will return to normal. The presentations will start, so you have to be ready. Thank you both – for everything!"

Rachel and Kirsty dashed out of the

staff room and ran back the way they had come. When they reached the ICT centre, the Mayor, the press and all the pupils were gathering for the presentation ceremony. As soon as Rachel and Kirsty had found seats, the teachers arrived with the folder full of certificates.

"I am very proud to be able to award

the ICT centre's very first certificates," said the headmaster.

He called out the names of the pupils and they stepped up to the stage to receive their awards. The crowd clapped and cameras flashed, but when Rachel and Kirsty's turn came, they saw a different kind of light in the crowd. For a moment, Tilly the Teacher Fairy hovered behind the crowds, smiling. She blew them a kiss, and then she vanished in a puff of silvery fairy dust.

"Well done," said Kirsty, giving her best

friend a hug. "You should be really proud."

"Well done to you too," said Rachel.

"I *am* proud of our certificates...but it means even more that we've been able to help our fairy friends again!"

Now it's time for Kirsty and
Rachel to help...

Marissa the Science Fairy

Read on for a sneak peek...

Kirsty Tate smoothed down the jacket of
her new school uniform and bit her lip.

"I feel excited one minute and nervous
the next!" she said.

Her best friend, Rachel Walker, laughed
and hugged her.

"Stop worrying," she said. "Just think
how exciting it is that we are going
to school together for a whole week!
And you look really smart in my
spare uniform."

It was the first day of the new term, and
they were on their way to school. After
weeks of late-summer storms and bad

weather, Kirsty's school in Wetherbury had been flooded. It was going to take a week to get back to normal, and in the meantime her parents had agreed that she could stay with the Walkers. Best of all, she could go to Tippington School with Rachel!

"It's just a bit scary going to a new school," said Kirsty.

"But you'll be with me, in all the same lessons," Rachel reminded her. "Besides, we always have fun when we're together, don't we?"

Rachel always knew how to cheer her best friend up.

"I have the best times with you," Kirsty replied with a laugh. "We've had lots of fun adventures with the fairies, haven't we? Oh, Rachel, wouldn't it be amazing if our fairy friends visited us at school!"

Ever since the girls had met on Rainspell Island, they had kept the secret of their friendship with the fairies. They had often visited Fairyland together, and the fairies had taken them on many magical adventures in the human world.

"Look,!" said Rachel, noticing three people waving at them from further down the street. It was her friends Adam, Amina and Ellie.

"Hi, Rachel!" they called. "Hi, Kirsty!"

Kirsty had met them on one of her visits, and when they smiled at her she instantly felt more comfortable.

"Have you moved to Tippington?" asked Amina in an excited voice. "Ooh, I hope so!"

"Not exactly," said Kirsty with a laugh. "My school got flooded, so I'm staying with Rachel until it's fixed."

"Well I hope it takes ages," said Ellie
with a grin.

"Me too," said Rachel. Kirsty had a
feeling that going to school with Rachel
was going to be really good fun!

Read **Marissa the Science Fairy** to
find out what adventures are in store for Kirsty and Rachel!

Join in the magic online by signing up to
the Rainbow Magic fan club!

Sign up today at:
www.rainbowmagicbooks.co.uk

Have you read them all?

The Rainbow Fairies
1. Ruby the Red Fairy ☑
2. Amber the Orange Fairy ☐
3. Saffron the Yellow Fairy ☐
4. Fern the Green Fairy ☑
5. Sky the Blue Fairy ☐
6. Izzy the Indigo Fairy ☐
7. Heather the Violet Fairy ☑

The Weather Fairies
8. Crystal the Snow Fairy ☐
9. Abigail the Breeze Fairy ☐
10. Pearl the Cloud Fairy ☐
11. Goldie the Sunshine Fairy ☐
12. Evie the Mist Fairy ☑
13. Storm the Lightning Fairy ☐
14. Hayley the Rain Fairy ☐

The Party Fairies
15. Cherry the Cake Fairy ☐
16. Melodie the Music Fairy ☐
17. Grace the Glitter Fairy ☐
18. Honey the Sweet Fairy ☐
19. Polly the Party Fun Fairy ☐
20. Phoebe the Fashion Fairy ☐
21. Jasmine the Present Fairy ☐

The Jewel Fairies
22. India the Moonstone Fairy ☐
23. Scarlett the Garnet Fairy ☐
24. Emily the Emerald Fairy ☐
25. Chloe the Topaz Fairy ☐
26. Amy the Amethyst Fairy ☐
27. Sophie the Sapphire Fairy ☐
28. Lucy the Diamond Fairy ☐

The Pet Keeper Fairies
29. Katie the Kitten Fairy ☐
30. Bella the Bunny Fairy ☑
31. Georgia the Guinea Pig Fairy ☐
32. Lauren the Puppy Fairy ☐
33. Harriet the Hamster Fairy ☐
34. Molly the Goldfish Fairy ☐
35. Penny the Pony Fairy ☐

The Fun Day Fairies
36. Megan the Monday Fairy ☐
37. Tallulah the Tuesday Fairy ☐
38. Willow the Wednesday Fairy ☐
39. Thea the Thursday Fairy ☐
40. Freya the Friday Fairy ☐
41. Sienna the Saturday Fairy ☐
42. Sarah the Sunday Fairy ☐

The Petal Fairies
43. Tia the Tulip Fairy ☐
44. Pippa the Poppy Fairy ☐
45. Louise the Lily Fairy ☐
46. Charlotte the Sunflower Fairy ☐
47. Olivia the Orchid Fairy ☐
48. Danielle the Daisy Fairy ☐
49. Ella the Rose Fairy ☐

The Dance Fairies
50. Bethany the Ballet Fairy ☐
51. Jade the Disco Fairy ☐
52. Rebecca the Rock'n'Roll Fairy ☐
53. Tasha the Tap Dance Fairy ☐
54. Jessica the Jazz Fairy ☐
55. Saskia the Salsa Fairy ☐
56. Imogen the Ice Dance Fairy ☐

The Sporty Fairies
57. Helena the Horseriding Fairy ☐
58. Francesca the Football Fairy ☐
59. Zoe the Skating Fairy ☐
60. Naomi the Netball Fairy ☐
61. Samantha the Swimming Fairy ☐
62. Alice the Tennis Fairy ☐
63. Gemma the Gymnastics Fairy ☐

The Music Fairies
64. Poppy the Piano Fairy ☐
65. Ellie the Guitar Fairy ☐
66. Fiona the Flute Fairy ☐
67. Danni the Drum Fairy ☐
68. Maya the Harp Fairy ☐
69. Victoria the Violin Fairy ☐
70. Sadie the Saxophone Fairy ☐

The Magical Animal Fairies

71. Ashley the Dragon Fairy ☐
72. Lara the Black Cat Fairy ☑
73. Erin the Firebird Fairy ☑
74. Rihanna the Seahorse Fairy ☐
75. Sophia the Snow Swan Fairy ☐
76. Leona the Unicorn Fairy ☑
77. Caitlin the Ice Bear Fairy ☑

The Green Fairies

78. Nicole the Beach Fairy ☐
79. Isabella the Air Fairy ☐
80. Edie the Garden Fairy ☐
81. Coral the Reef Fairy ☐
82. Lily the Rainforest Fairy ☐
83. Carrie the Snow Cap Fairy ☑
84. Milly the River Fairy ☐

The Ocean Fairies

85. Ally the Dolphin Fairy ☐
86. Amelie the Seal Fairy ☐
87. Pia the Penguin Fairy ☐
88. Tess the Sea Turtle Fairy ☑
89. Stephanie the Starfish Fairy ☐
90. Whitney the Whale Fairy ☑
91. Courtney the Clownfish Fairy ☐

The Twilight Fairies

92. Ava the Sunset Fairy ☑
93. Lexi the Firefly Fairy ☐
94. Zara the Starlight Fairy ☐
95. Morgan the Midnight Fairy ☐
96. Yasmin the Night Owl Fairy ☐
97. Maisie the Moonbeam Fairy ☐
98. Sabrina the Sweet Dreams Fairy ☐

The Showtime Fairies

99. Madison the Magic Show Fairy ☐
100. Leah the Theatre Fairy ☐
101. Alesha the Acrobat Fairy ☐
102. Darcey the Dance Diva Fairy ☐
103. Taylor the Talent Show Fairy ☐
104. Amelia the Singing Fairy ☐
105. Isla the Ice Star Fairy ☐

The Princess Fairies

106. Honor the Happy Days Fairy ☐
107. Demi the Dressing-Up Fairy ☐
108. Anya the Cuddly Creatures Fairy ☐
109. Elisa the Adventure Fairy ☐
110. Lizzie the Sweet Treats Fairy ☐
111. Maddie the Playtime Fairy ☐
112. Eva the Enchanted Ball Fairy ☐

The Pop Star Fairies

113. Jessie the Lyrics Fairy ☐
114. Adele the Singing Coach Fairy ☐
115. Vanessa the Dance Steps Fairy ☑
116. Miley the Stylist Fairy ☐
117. Frankie the Make-Up Fairy ☐
118. Rochelle the Star Spotter Fairy ☐
119. Una the Concert Fairy ☐

The Fashion Fairies

120. Miranda the Beauty Fairy ☐
121. Claudia the Accessories Fairy ☐
122. Tyra the Dress Designer Fairy ☐
123. Alexa the Fashion Reporter Fairy ☐
124. Matilda the Hair Stylist Fairy ☐
125. Brooke the Photographer Fairy ☐
126. Lola the Fashion Fairy ☐

The Sweet Fairies

127. Lottie the Lollipop Fairy ☑
128. Esme the Ice Cream Fairy ☐
129. Coco the Cupcake Fairy ☐
130. Clara the Chocolate Fairy ☐
131. Madeleine the Cookie Fairy ☐
132. Layla the Candyfloss Fairy ☐
133. Nina the Birthday Cake Fairy ☐

The Baby Animal Rescue Fairies

134. Mae the Panda Fairy ☐
135. Kitty the Tiger Fairy ☐
136. Mara the Meerkat Fairy ☐
137. Savannah the Zebra Fairy ☐
138. Kimberley the Koala Fairy ☐
139. Rosie the Honey Bear Fairy ☐
140. Anna the Arctic Fox Fairy ☐

The Magical Crafts Fairies

141. Kayla the Pottery Fairy ☐
142. Annabelle the Drawing Fairy ☐
143. Zadie the Sewing Fairy ☐
144. Josie the Jewellery-Making Fairy ☐
145. Violet the Painting Fairy ☐
146. Libby the Story-Writing Fairy ☐
147. Roxie the Baking Fairy ☐

There's a book of fairy fun for everyone!

www.rainbowmagicbooks.co.uk

Giselle the Christmas Ballet Fairy

Meet Giselle the Christmas Ballet Fairy! Can Rachel and Kirsty help get her magical items back from Jack Frost in time for the Fairyland Christmas Eve performance?

www.rainbowmagicbooks.co.uk